Lavender Finds a Friend

Based on the Original Flower Fairies™ Books
by Cicely Mary Barker

Frederick Warne

Hidden amongst the leaves
and blossoms in the garden,
the flower fairies live quietly.
At night, they come out to play!

In the morning, a sleepy Lavender is the first to wake up. She has lots to do! She sings to the other garden fairies, to wake them up, too!

Lavender's blue diddle, diddle—
Lavender's green;
I'll scent the clothes diddle diddle
Put away clean—
Clean from the wash, diddle diddle,
Hanky and sheet;
Lavender's spikes, diddle diddle,
Make them all sweet.

When Lavender
has a minute to spare,
she writes in
her diary.

Dear Diary

Today I have been busy
washing the fairies' clothes.
I have made some soft

lavender soap

and I scrub away
at the stains. I wonder
what some of the
fairies get up to – their
clothes are so dirty!

Once Lavender finishes washing
the fairies' clothes, she hangs them
up on the line to dry.
"Your bonnet is beautifully scented!"
says Sweet Pea Fairy to her sister.

One day, in the garden, Lavender hears two fairy friends laughing together.

"I wish I had a best friend of my own," Lavender thinks.

That evening
Lavender writes
in her diary...

Dear Diary

I'm sad tonight.

Every day I wash an

scent the fairies' cott

but I never

have time to make

any friends. My only
friends are the white

butterflies who visit each day

to drink Lavender nectar.

Whatever shall I do?

"I know what I'll do,
I'll make a friendly fairy spell,"
says Lavender.
This is what
she puts in it:

a dash of
fairy dust

a whisper
of moon sparkle

a drop
of dew

a tiny fairy
giggle

a sprinkle of
Lavender petals

Lavender casts the spell and
waits to see who will come…

Out steps Cornflower from the
flower bed. "I'll be your friend!" he says.
"Me too!" calls Foxglove from behind her.
"And me," says Snapdragon.
Lavender laughs.
"What a wonderful spell!" she says.

FREDERICK WARNE

Published by the Penguin Group
Penguin Books Ltd, 80 Strand, London WC2R 0RL, England
New York, Australia, Canada, India, New Zealand, South Africa

This edition first published by Frederick Warne 2003
1 3 5 7 9 10 8 6 4 2

ISBN 0 7232 489

Printed in China